Other Apple Paperbacks
you might enjoy:

The Mystery Hideout
by Ken Follett

The Ghost in the Noonday Sun
by Sid Fleischman

The Haunting
by Margaret Mahy

The Computer That Ate My Brother
by Dean Marney

The Hidden Treasure
by John Rowe Townsend

I Spent My Summer Vacation Kidnapped into Space
by Martyn Godfrey

The POWER TWINS

KEN FOLLETT

Illustrated by Stephen Marchesi

AN
APPLE
PAPERBACK

SCHOLASTIC INC.
New York Toronto London Auckland Sydney

Previously published in England as *The Power Twins and the Worm Puzzle*, 1976.

ISBN 0-590-42507-2

12 11 10 9 8 7 6 5 4 3 2 1   1 2 3 4 5 6/9

Printed in the U.S.A.   28

First Scholastic printing, September 1991

CONTENTS

· ·

ONE

· ·

UNCLE WHO?

▼

"I didn't know we had an Uncle Grigorian," said Fritz Price.

"It's a funny name," said his twin sister, Helen. "Are you sure you've got it right, Tubs?"

"Don't call me Tubs," said Tubs.

The twins were sitting on the low brick wall at the front of Sunnyview, the seaside guesthouse which Mrs. Price ran. The house did not really have a view, unless you counted the row of guesthouses just like Sunnyview on the opposite side of the street. However, it was sunny, being the end of July.

They had just had lunch, and while they were making up their minds what to do for the afternoon, they were watching Saturday's new

arrivals draw up, their cars loaded to the luggage racks with suitcases, folding chairs, thermos flasks, buckets, and spades.

In fact, Helen and Fritz had been trying to think of a way of avoiding Tubs for the rest of the day. He was their cousin, three years younger than they, and, as Fritz kept saying, he was a little fat pain in the neck. It was always the same when he came to spend the summer holidays at Sunnyview. At first the twins went out of their way to be nice to him: took him swimming in the evenings when the beach was less crowded, included him in their games of cricket in the sunshine and Monopoly in the rain, and showed him their secret den in the brambles on the cliff walk where you could watch the rabbits.

Then, after a few days, they began to get tired of his childishness and tried to ignore him. That always made him demand to be included in everything in a loud, shrill voice, and the twins always ended up trying to escape from him.

That was what they had been planning when he had come out of the house—having taken longer over his lunch than anyone else, as usual—and announced that Uncle Grigorian was coming. Like most of their conversations with Tubs, it led quickly to a quarrel about his nickname.

"My name's Jonathan," Tubs added.

"Fritz's real name is Richard," Helen said, "but he doesn't complain." Fritz had a patch of hair at the front which would do nothing but stick straight up into the air. He did not like his nickname, but he was old enough to know that if you make a fuss about a thing like that, people do it even more.

There had been a time when he had spent hours in front of the mirror, trying to make the hair go flat with brushes, water, and Brylcream; but it had not worked. Nowadays his hair was quite long at the sides, and with the sticking-up bit at the front he looked like Rod Stewart, so he quite liked it.

"Besides," said Fritz, "I can't help my hair, but you could lose weight."

"Well, I've got another nickname now," Tubs said with a sneer.

"What?"

"The Ringo Kid." With that Tubs drew an imaginary gun from an imaginary holster, shot both his cousins, and galloped back into the house on an imaginary horse.

"Blimey, five more weeks of this," Fritz groaned.

"Let's go and find out about this uncle," Helen suggested.

They jumped off the wall and walked across the front garden, which was not a garden at all but a parking lot for the guests. The house was packed with guests, going in and out with their luggage and finding the bathrooms, the television lounge, and the dining room. They found their mother upstairs making a bed.

She was wearing a nylon sweater and trousers, which made her look plain. When she dressed up and put on some makeup, she looked quite attractive. She always said she was twenty-one, which Fritz thought was a very silly deception, since it was obvious she must be forty or fifty or something.

As soon as they walked in she said, "Do the other side of this bed with me, Helen. Janice is downstairs and Mrs. Williams would choose Saturday to have one of her turns." Janice and Mrs. Williams were the staff of the guesthouse, not counting Frank Cheesewright, who did odd jobs and sometimes took Mrs. Price to the movies in the winter.

Helen started tucking in sheets while Fritz tried to make himself useful by emptying one wastepaper basket into another.

"Have we really got an Uncle Grigorian coming?" Helen asked.

"Yes, and I hope to goodness he won't want to stay the night, because I've already had one family turn up with two more children than expected and I haven't a clue where I'm going to put them."

"How come we haven't heard of him before?" asked Fritz. "Where does he live? Why is he coming here?"

Mrs. Price plumped up the pillows and started on the second bed. "He lives on a farm in Wales, and I've no idea why he's coming here. He said he wants to see us."

"But why have we never heard of him?" Fritz repeated.

A pretty young woman only a few years older than Helen came in with a cup of tea in her hand.

"Oh, Janice, bless your heart. Just what I need," said Mrs. Price. She sat down on the edge of the bed and stirred her tea while the twins waited patiently for her to explain about the mysterious uncle.

"We've only met him once," she began. "That was at your father's funeral. You wouldn't remember." Her voice took on a sort of brisk, businesslike tone which it always had when she mentioned the twins' father. He had died in a car crash when they were very small, and Mrs. Price had bought the guesthouse with money from the life insurance policies.

"Your father was never sure how many brothers he had," she went on. "You know the family was all split up in Poland during the war. Daddy was more or less an orphan when he came here, and he never heard from his family. Anyway, when he died, Uncle Grigorian saw the notice in a paper and came to the funeral. He lived in Germany in those days, but he happened to be in England on business at the time.

"He was very nice to me. Offered to help me out financially, but I didn't need it. After the funeral I never saw him again. Now, it seems, he's living in Britain and wants to see us all again. I can't remember quite what he looks like."

And the explanation, as Fritz remarked to Helen afterward, made Uncle Grigorian all the more mysterious.

As it turned out, he had funny thumbs. It was Helen who noticed them first. They grew from a point near the middle of the base of the hand, instead of from the side. When Tubs noticed it, after Helen had pointed it out, he said that Uncle Grigorian was a Man from Outer Space, and proceeded to shoot Fritz with an imaginary ray blaster.

However, apart from the thumbs he was just what an uncle ought to be. He had a beard and moustache and twinkling eyes, he dressed in a suit with a vest, and he was rather short.

Fritz was more interested in his car, which was a red Triumph. Fritz said it had fuel injection and went like a bomb.

Helen said, "Frank Cheesewright says one car is as good as another, so long as it starts when you switch it on and doesn't stop until you switch it off."

"That's because he's only got a secondhand Ford, and he knows less about cars than you do," Fritz retorted. The twins bickered quite a lot, and although they would never admit it, they got on best when Tubs was around to be nagged by both of them.

This particular argument was stopped before it got started by Janice, who called them in for tea. The family had tea early at Sunnyview, so as to get it out of the way before the guests' dinner at half-past six. Today they had ham and salad, in honor of Uncle Grigorian, who ate dozens of new potatoes.

While he was drinking tea and demolishing a lot of bread and butter and honey, he told them about his farm. "It's half a mountain, in fact," he said with a grin. "I've got several hundred sheep, whose main job is to keep the grass down. I keep a few pigs, which are no trouble until they escape. Then they're the devil to catch."

Helen giggled at the thought of short, stubby Uncle Grigorian waddling about a farmyard trying to catch a runaway pig.

After tea he rolled up his shirt-sleeves, put on a flowered apron, and insisted on washing the dishes. The children were helping to clear away, so they heard him say to Mrs. Price, "I've got a room at the Grand, down on the promenade, for tonight."

"I'm sorry I can't offer you a bed here," she replied. "But we're full up. . . ."

"Of course you are, at this time of year."

"In fact we're more than full. I could do with another room this week. I still don't know where I'm going to put a couple of extra guests who've turned up."

"Really?" He seemed to think that very interesting. "Actually, that would fit in rather well with some plans of my own—if you agree to them."

Mrs. Price stopped ladling canned fruit into dessert dishes and looked at him.

"I was wondering," he said, "whether the twins would like to come and stay with me for a few days. I'd like to see more of them—get to know them—now that I'm in Britain to live. It would take them off your hands while you're so busy, and of course you would then have the extra bedroom you need."

She looked a bit doubtful. "I'm afraid they can't desert Jonathan. He's here for the holidays, and it wouldn't be polite for them to go away and leave their cousin on his own."

"Tubs can come, too," Uncle Grigorian said. "I wouldn't dream of leaving him out."

"I'd have to ask my sister."

"Does she have a telephone?"

"Yes. I'll call her."

While she went out to phone, Uncle Grigorian turned to the children. He had a very slight foreign accent, which came out more strongly when he spoke to them. "What do you think of the idea?" he asked. "You must tell me if you think you wouldn't like it. It's only a farm, after all. But you can help round up the sheep, and drive the tractors, and wander around in the fields. If you feel energetic, we could go for walks over the mountains.

"You can stay as long as you like. And as soon as you get fed up with it, I'll drive you back here."

"It sounds great!" said Helen, who was mad about animals.

"Me, too," Fritz put in. He would have gone a thousand miles for a chance to drive a tractor.

"And me," said Tubs, who did not want to be left out of anything.

Mrs. Price came back into the kitchen. "Jonathan's mother is quite happy about it," she said. "Do you have a phone, Grigorian?"

"Of course. I'll make sure the children call you every evening."

"Oh, there's no need for that. Just as long as I can keep in touch. When would you like to leave?"

"Well, you need that spare room tonight, don't you?"

"Yes, but you're booked in at the Grand. . . ."

"Don't worry about that. I don't much like the place anyway. If they don't take too long packing, we can be there by ten o'clock tonight."

And the whole unbelievable adventure started as simply as that.

TWO

. . . .

SOME FARM—
SOME FARMER!

_____

▼

*T*he sound of sheep baaing woke Fritz up. He looked around at the white walls, the tiny window, and the huge double bed he was in; and the events of yesterday flooded back into his mind.

He had packed his case in record time, throwing in a spare pair of jeans, a parka and Wellingtons in case of rain, a couple of sweaters and some underwear.

The ride in the Triumph had been terrific. Uncle Grigorian did not seem to know about speed limits, and the speedometer needle had touched 80 on the superhighway.

When they had arrived at the farm there had been a hot drink and a mountain of chocolate cookies; then they had all gone to bed. Fritz's last thought before sleep had been that if all uncles were like this about speed limits and chocolate cookies, he wished he had more of them.

He jumped out of bed and went to the tiny window. The bedroom was chilly, but outside it was another sunny day. The big farmhouse was built on a slope, facing down the hillside, and Fritz's bedroom was at the back, so that, although you went downstairs to get out of the front of the house, the yard at the rear was on a level with the bedroom floor.

The yard was surrounded by rather dilapidated old stone buildings. Beyond them the coarse grass rose steeply to the top of a small mountain—or a large hill, depending on how you looked at it.

Fritz went to the washbasin in the corner and splashed water on his face, just so that he would be able to say he had washed if anyone asked. He had a feeling that Uncle Grigorian wouldn't ask.

He went downstairs to find everyone else up and digging into a breakfast served by a fat, bustling lady called Mrs. Rhys.

Uncle Grigorian explained, "Mrs. Rhys looks after this house and her husband runs the farm."

"What do you do, then?" asked Tubs, who was always coming out with things like that.

Uncle Grigorian laughed. "I plan to spend the rest of the day telling you about that," he said. "Eat up, now."

People seemed to eat a lot on farms, Fritz decided. Mrs. Rhys brought him an enormous plate of bacon, sausage, two fried eggs, baked beans, tomatoes, mushrooms, and fried bread.

Uncle Grigorian lit up a big pipe while the others were finishing their breakfast. "Today is a day of surprises," he said. "But first, I have some promises to keep. Driving lessons for Fritz and Tubs, and a look at the lambs for Helen."

Helen went off up the mountainside with Mr. Rhys, a tall Welshman in a cap and Wellington boots; and Fritz and Tubs went out to the farmyard.

Uncle Grigorian threw open a barn door to reveal a tractor, with mud all over its red paint. He sat Fritz in the seat and showed him how to put it into first gear. Then he started the engine.

"Off you go!" he shouted above the roar.

Fritz shoved the lever forward and the tractor rumbled slowly out of the barn into the yard. In no time at all he found himself heading for a stone wall. He yanked the wheel around—it was harder than he expected—and steered around the yard.

Uncle Grigorian opened the farmyard gate and pointed through it. Fritz steered between the gateposts and out onto the track beyond. The others ran after him.

Eventually Uncle Grigorian motioned him to stop, and he pulled back the lever.

"Tubs's turn," said Uncle Grigorian. "I'll turn her around." He clambered up into the metal seat and did a three-point turn. He seemed to enjoy it as much as Fritz had.

Then Tubs got behind the wheel and was given the same set of instructions. With a wide beam of pleasure on his face, he drove off down the track toward the farmyard.

"I suppose it will go faster," said Fritz as they half-walked, half-ran behind.

"Yes. I'll show you how to accelerate another day," puffed Uncle Grigorian.

Tubs reached forward over the wheel to a lever.

"Don't touch that!" Uncle Grigorian shouted.

Tubs tugged at it. Suddenly the tractor shot forward. Tubs rocked back, almost falling backward off the machine, which swerved wildly up the slope beside the track. Uncle Grigorian ran faster, caught up with the tractor, and jumped on behind. He leaned past Tubs and pushed the lever forward. The tractor slowed down and entered the farmyard.

"Trust you," said Fritz breathlessly as Tubs climbed down.

Uncle Grigorian laughed. "I didn't show you

the brake because I didn't show you the throttle," he said. "I might have guessed you'd find it yourself."

"You couldn't know what he's like," Fritz said.

"Ah," Uncle Grigorian replied. "I know more about you than you might think."

Fritz was about to ask what he meant, but Helen came back. "They're gorgeous," she said. "All fluffy and playful."

Uncle Grigorian clapped his hands. "Right," he said. "Now I want to show you something. This way."

He led them across the yard to one of the stone buildings. It was not as dilapidated as the rest. It had no windows, and its door looked sound. He opened it with a key, let them in, switched on the light, and closed the door.

The room looked just like a modern office. There was gray wall-to-wall carpeting on the floor, white-painted walls, three easy chairs, a desk, a swivel chair, a filing cabinet, and a typewriter.

"What's so special about an office?" asked Tubs in his usual blunt manner.

"You'll see," said Uncle Grigorian.

Fritz wondered why he was making such a fuss about the place. "Is this where you do your work?"

"You might say that, yes," Uncle Grigorian

replied. He seemed determined to be mysterious about the whole thing.

Helen was examining the door. "This is odd," she said.

Fritz went over. "What?"

"Look, I can't get my fingernail in the crack of the door. It must be a very tight fit. How does any air get in here?"

Fritz looked closer. He touched the door. His finger stopped a millimeter short of the wood. There seemed to be a thin layer of clear plastic stuff over the door. He ran his finger along to the wall. "It's like a seal, all around the room!" he exclaimed.

"Correct," Uncle Grigorian said. "Now let me show you what it's for."

He opened the filing cabinet. Instead of pulling out a drawer, he swung the whole of the front open, revealing a set of switches and dials. He twiddled for a moment, then shut the door.

"Notice anything?"

Helen looked around. "The walls have gone dark," she said.

"Just a minute." He walked over to the light switch. "Sit down, all of you. You don't want to bump into each other in the dark." They obeyed, and he turned the light off. "Look up!"

When they did, they could see the stars— millions of them, far more than usual, and brighter. There was something else in the sky:

a huge planet, blue in color, dressed in wisps of clouds. A slim crescent of it was in darkness.

"We're on the moon!" Tubs shouted excitedly.

"Don't be crazy," said Fritz. "It's a projection—the Earth, seen from space. It's incredibly good."

"It's beautiful," Helen whispered.

Suddenly Fritz noticed something. "The walls," he said.

"They're dark," said Tubs.

"Look through them, not at them."

The three children strained their eyes. They could see a gray, uneven landscape, a bit like a moonlit desert, with hills in the distance.

"I told you—we're on the moon," repeated Tubs.

Uncle Grigorian switched the light on, and the walls became opaque again. The stars, too, disappeared, but the Earth was still visible on the ceiling.

"What do you think?" asked Uncle Grigorian.

"It's very clever," said Fritz. He frowned.

"Wondering how it's done?"

"Yes. It's easy with the roof, and three of the walls. All you need is a back projector behind this clear plastic stuff. But the front wall—where the door is—has just got the yard behind it."

"It's much simpler than that," said Uncle Grigorian. "We are on the moon."

Fritz gave a bit of a laugh. That was the kind of joke you expected from Tubs. "You don't expect us to believe you, do you?" he asked.

"Not until I've proved it," said Uncle Grigorian seriously.

Tubs said, "Take a walk outside—that'll prove it."

"We can't, of course," Fritz said. "We can't open the door—even if we knew just where it was."

"Fair enough," said Uncle Grigorian. He re-opened his filing cabinet, made some more adjustments, and suddenly the walls and the door of the stone farmyard building were back again. "Let's go somewhere else," he said.

This time the walls and the ceiling stayed the same, but a window appeared beside the door. Fritz looked out of it.

"Trafalgar Square!"

Uncle Grigorian just smiled again.

"The walls are very thick," Fritz said. "You could have a projector embedded in the stone."

"But here you can go outside," Uncle Grigorian replied.

Fritz looked at him.

"Go on!"

"All right," he agreed. It would be worth it to put an end to this prolonged joke.

He opened the door, stepped out, and found himself on the pavement in Trafalgar Square.

He stopped dead on the pavement, his mouth hanging open in astonishment. He had fully expected to step into the farmyard. His heart seemed to thump like a hammer in his chest as he stared numbly at Nelson's Column, rising high in the air in front of him.

A man in a derby bumped into him. Fritz apologized, and pulled himself together. He looked carefully around him. On the far side of Nelson's Column, just where it should be, was the unmistakable front of the National Gallery. The roar of the traffic was in his ears, and his nose wrinkled at the stale smell of the London air. He took a tentative step forward, as if to check that the pavement was solid. Nothing happened, except that he was one pace nearer to the curb.

He turned around to see where he had come from. Instead of a stone farm building, he saw an anonymous-looking door with a dark window beside it, squeezed in between a shop window and a movie theater entrance. There were no markings on the door to show where it led, and if you walked past it you would hardly notice it was there.

On the nearest corner, beside the Charing Cross station, a man was selling the evening papers. Fritz walked across to him, gave him five pence, and took a paper. It was the racing edition. Fritz looked at the date. It was today's.

Feeling rather dazed, he walked back to the door, pushed it open, and stepped into the office. He gave the newspaper to Helen and sat down.

"Well," he said eventually, "if you can go to London, I suppose you can go to the moon."

THREE

. . . .

THE POWERS

▼

"In fact, it's easier to go to the moon than to London," Uncle Grigorian said. "I suppose this is what is called a spaceship. It consists of this clear plastic wall"—he waved his hand to indicate the whole room—"and the drive unit." He patted the filing cabinet. "Moving around is easy—I just have to press a button, and I'm there. But I have to say exactly where I want to go.

"That's the hard part. It's not so bad on the moon, where I don't have to worry about accidentally bumping into something. But to shift to this place, in Trafalgar Square, I have to give precise space-time coordinates."

"I see," Fritz said. "I suppose you found this

room first, rented it, locked it up—"

"Correct. It had to be roughly the same size as my ship, in case anyone should get in while I'm here. If there was a three-inch gap between the wall of the ship and the wall of the room, for example, it might give me away."

"You must have to recalculate the coordinates each time, because the Earth is always moving."

"It's not that bad. After the first time, the computer in here"—he patted the filing cabinet again—"adjusts the coordinates continuously."

Fritz was fascinated. "So all you have to do is find a room roughly the size of the ship, plot its position, and feed the figures in. After that you can go there any time you like. Is it instantaneous?"

"Virtually, on Earth at any rate. Traveling through space, it takes long enough to notice."

Helen broke in. "Have you got rooms anywhere else, other than Wales and London?"

"Yes." He moved a dial and said, "Now look out."

Helen saw that they were now very high up. The window had become much bigger. The city they were in was a forest of skyscrapers.

"New York," she said, remembering pictures in geography books.

"Chicago, actually," said Uncle Grigorian. He pressed another button. They saw Tokyo,

Caracas, Vienna, Leningrad, and Hong Kong, all in the space of a few minutes. In each city the window was a different shape, and the office was at a different height. Sometimes the door went out onto the pavement, and sometimes it was on the opposite wall and led to a corridor and an elevator or a staircase.

In the end the children called a halt. Helen said, "I feel as if I've eaten too much ice cream, or something."

"How on earth does it work? I mean, what drives the engine?" said Fritz.

"I've no idea," Uncle Grigorian replied. "I'm not a physicist."

"Then—" Fritz gulped, and started the question again. "Uncle Grigorian, what are you?"

Uncle Grigorian insisted on going back to Wales and getting some lunch before he answered the question. They went into the farmhouse kitchen and found the table laid with slices of cold roast beef, two huge pieces of cheese, and a couple of loaves of fresh bread. Surprised to see that it was after two o'clock, they all filled their plates and settled down to eat.

"Now," said Uncle Grigorian, "I said it was going to be a day of surprises, so here's number two. I'm not your uncle."

They all stopped eating and stared at him.

"I needed a family to sort of attach myself to, and yours was ideal," he continued. "It's one of the few families in which someone can turn up and claim to be a relative, and no one can be sure he's not. Well, I turned up ten years ago, as your mother has probably told you. I intended to see a lot more of all of you, but shortly afterward the nature of my work changed, and I dropped the project."

"What is your work?" Helen asked.

"That will become clear eventually. For now, call me a sociologist."

"What happened to change your mind— about attaching yourself to our family again, I mean," Helen persisted.

"I got a special request from my government," he said. "They need your help."

That didn't really make much sense to any of them. Tubs asked, "Where do you come from, then?"

Uncle Grigorian paused. "My home," he said, "is called Klipst. It's seventeen light-years away, near a small star called Marn." He paused again, then smiled. "That's surprise number three."

"The funny thumbs!" Helen said. Then she blushed.

Fritz said, "Tubs said you were a Man from Outer Space."

"Tubs is right about more things than you

give him credit for," said Uncle Grigorian. "However, I'd better tell you the whole thing before you start worrying.

"I told you I'm a sociologist, and it is part of the truth. I study societies. But I also work for the government—the Galactic Empire, I suppose you'd call it—as a sort of secret agent.

"I have to keep an eye on a number of worlds which are on the verge of discovering space travel. Earth is one of them."

"We've already discovered it," Fritz put in.

"No, this rocketry business doesn't count. Your scientists have gone up a bit of a blind alley with that. But it won't be long before they discover the hyperdrive. And when they do, the government will need to know that there is a new world ready to be admitted to the community of planets."

Helen asked, "Where do we come in?"

"There's a dispute in what we call the Genic Sector. My government got the two sides to agree to have the question decided by an independent body, but they could not find anyone independent enough. Eventually, in desperation, they decided to pull in someone from a world outside the Empire.

"They also decided that the arbitrators must not be adults—apparently no adult is capable of being completely unbiased. As in this world, politicians have a way of coming up with grandiose schemes and leaving the details to other people to sort out. This problem landed on my boss's desk, and he passed it to me."

"You mean we've got to sit here and make a decision about some dispute in outer space?" Fritz was incredulous.

"Not sit here. You'll have to come with me to Palassan—the capital of the Galactic Empire."

"Blimey!" said Fritz. It was all he could think of to say.

"It's not as crazy as it sounds," Uncle Grigorian went on. "It's a well-known fact that youngsters have a finer sense of justice than adults." He smiled. "We're too hardened to the unfairness of life, or something, I suppose. Anyway, that's all by-the-way. You're supposed to be staying with me for two weeks, and it won't take that long. The phone in the farmhouse will reach us anywhere in the Milky Way, so you can keep in touch with your mother. The question is, will you do it?"

Tubs said, "You bet!" and buttered himself another slice of bread.

Fritz and Helen looked at one another. Helen said, "I think we both would like to help, but we're just not sure we can do the job."

"Let me worry about that," said Uncle Grigorian. "I've found out a lot about you three in the last few months. I know you're clever and fair-minded. Besides, I'm going to give you some help, which I can't tell you about until I'm sure you agree to go."

They looked at one another again. Then they both said, "We'll go." Fritz added, "Tell us what help we'll get."

"I'm going to give you the Powers," he said. "It's a kind of mental weapon. You have to have special treatment, but it can be done in your sleep.

"It's only been discovered recently, and it's enormously expensive, so only a handful of people in the whole Galactic Empire have had it. I'm not one of them, by the way."

"How does it work?"

"You can never be sure in advance. Basically, it gives an enormous boost to whatever intellectual skills you already have. If you already have a talent for numbers, say, it would turn you into a brilliant mathematician. But it's usually more general than that. We have names for the different kinds of result. However, we'll go into that when you've had the treatment."

Tubs said, "I'll be a kung-fu killer," and made chopping movements with his hands.

Uncle Grigorian laughed. "I hope not," he said. "That would be fatal for all of us."

"It's all very confusing," said Fritz.

"Of course." Uncle Grigorian got up from the table. "You can have the treatment tonight, and we'll set off in the morning. Now, how about another driving lesson?"

Helen woke up with a sore ear. She put her hand to it and found the strange object, like a telephone earpiece, that Uncle Grigorian had taped there the previous night.

She sat up and looked around. The three of them had spent the night in the spaceship. Their earpieces were all connected to a little box, like a transistor radio. As she looked, Fritz and Tubs woke up.

"These chair beds are uncomfortable," Tubs said, and yawned.

There was a knock at the door and Uncle Grigorian walked in. Helen still thought of him as Uncle, even though she knew he was really no relation to them. He was carrying a tray with three glasses on it.

"Good morning, supermen," he said cheerfully. "You'll all need this drink."

It was warm and sweet and faintly scented, and Helen drank it all down. Uncle Grigorian sat on the edge of his desk. He looked quite excited.

"Well, let's find out how it worked," he said. "Fritz first. Feel any different?"

"Not really," Fritz said.

"Yes he does," Helen blurted out. "He just said that because he wants to know what happened to me and Tubs before he tells." Then she blushed at her outburst.

"Aha," said Uncle Grigorian. "How did you know that?"

"Well, when he said it, he put his arm up and scratched his head, and he had that kind of twist to his mouth and . . ."

"Enough!" said Uncle Grigorian. "You're a Reader. You can tell how people feel just by looking at them."

"A mind reader?" asked Tubs enviously.

"No. She reads bodies, not minds. There's a whole science, you know, of interpreting the little gestures people make—rubbing their noses, fingering their beards, the way they stand, put their hands in their pockets, all that sort of thing. Helen must have been quite good at guessing what people think before the treatment. Now she knows."

"Yes. You're jealous, I see," said Helen.

Uncle Grigorian laughed. "You'll have to learn to be tolerant now, Helen. Of course I'm jealous. Can't you see how useful it would be to me—as a sociologist—to be a Reader? However, let's get back to Fritz."

"All right," said Fritz. "It's only a small thing. But I went to bed wondering how we could get to Palassan. After all, if we went at the speed of light it would take over one hundred years."

"And this morning?"

"Well, now I can see how it might work. It's difficult to explain. . . ."

"Try."

"Look, then. Imagine a small, very flat creature. It's so thin, and so stupid, that it can't conceive the idea of up and down. All it knows is left or right, forward or backward. It never goes up and down, it can't see up and down, so it thinks in two dimensions.

"Now, the surface it lives on is like a sheet. The sheet might be flat, or it might be folded. Suppose it is folded. The creature will never find out.

"The creature travels around the surface of the sheet the whole of its life, never realizing that because the sheet is folded, it could take shortcuts by boring *down* or *up* through the material.

"Well, we are like that creature, only we think in three dimensions instead of two. But suppose space is folded in a fourth dimension? Then there would be shortcuts we could take by boring through the three-dimensional surface." He paused. "Now that I've said it, it doesn't seem so clear anymore."

"Never mind," said Uncle Grigorian. "We know what you are. You're a Synthesist. It means you can look at a set of facts and put them together very quickly. You could look at an engine and see instantly how it works; look at a chess game and understand the strategy of each player."

Fritz took off his earpiece and laid it down carefully beside the black box. "It's not the kind of Power I was expecting," he said. "I must say, it doesn't seem all that practical."

"You'll soon find out how useful it is. Now, how about Tubs?"

Tubs looked mournful. "I just did a karate chop on the arm of the chair, and all I did was hurt my hand," he said. The twins laughed.

"Don't you feel different in any way?"

"Nope."

Uncle Grigorian frowned. "I wonder," he said. He opened a drawer in his desk and took something out. It was round and about the size of a tennis ball. It had a surface of smooth, glistening fur, which looked a bit like sealskin.

"Catch," he said, and threw it to Tubs.

Tubs caught it and stroked the fur experimentally for a second. Then he put the thing up on his shoulder.

It seemed to settle into the curve of his neck, changing shape slightly.

Tubs said, "His name is Glob."

"I thought so," said Uncle Grigorian. "You're a Maverick. They always have an affinity for Petballs."

"Can I see?" Helen asked. She took the Pet-

ball from Tubs's shoulder and examined it. Its furry surface was unbroken. "It's just a ball of fur," she said, and gave it to Fritz.

"It's an animal, we think," said Uncle Grigorian. "They come from a strange planet on the far side of the galaxy. Nobody knows just how they live—there's no mouth, for example, nor even an eye—but live they do. People keep them as pets. They seem to like some people and dislike others. If they don't like you they simply fall off your shoulder. People who have the Maverick Power seem to get some kind of special rapport with Petballs. You saw how Tubs knew immediately that he had to put it on his shoulder and that its name was—what did you say, Tubs?"

"Glob."

"How did you know?"

"I don't know. It just came."

Fritz handed the Petball back to Tubs, who put it on his shoulder. "What sort of Power has Tubs got, then?" he asked.

"The most peculiar of all," Uncle Grigorian said. "It's got something to do with the odd habit he has of saying and doing unexpected things which often turn out to be right.

"He may not use his Power for months. But when he does, I guarantee you'll be grateful for it. Meanwhile, he's got Glob."

He picked up the tray and went to the door.

"I'll leave you to get dressed. Breakfast is almost ready. Oh, there's one other thing. The Empire has a sort of standard language. Everybody speaks it in the more advanced worlds, and even in the most primitive it's taught at school. It's rather like Earth's Esperanto."

"Oh!" said Helen. "How are we going to learn it?"

"It's part of the treatment you had in the night," Uncle Grigorian said with a grin. "You know it already. We've been speaking it for the last half hour."

He went out and shut the door.

. . . .

FOUR

HOP, SKIP, AND HYPERJUMP

▼

After breakfast the twins and Tubs packed their suitcases again and carried them into the office. Uncle Grigorian told Mrs. Rhys that they would be away for a few days, and he would telephone when they decided to come back. Then, when she had gone back to her own house, he drove his car into the garage and locked it.

"All set?" he asked as he came into the office. The three nodded impatiently. He opened his filing cabinet and set the dials.

"The journey will take almost an hour," he said. "We have to make short hops through ordinary space as well as jumps through hyperspace—what Fritz calls the fourth dimension.

The jumps themselves don't take very long—it's the pauses in between that delay us. There. We're off."

He closed the cabinet door and turned around. There was no sensation of movement at all, and for a moment Helen wondered whether something had gone wrong. But when she looked at the walls, she saw that the farm building had gone, leaving nothing but a very deep blackness on the other side of the clear plastic. As she watched, the scene changed again, and there was a distant sun through one wall and a sand-colored, dead-looking planet visible through the ceiling.

The changes came too quickly for her to take in the things that appeared outside the office—or spaceship, she should call it, she thought to herself. She gave up looking out.

Uncle Grigorian suggested some games to pass the time. He brought out a checkers set and arranged a tournament. Unfortunately, it turned out that Fritz could now beat everybody—including Uncle Grigorian—without even trying.

There was Monopoly, but they did not have enough time for that, so they divided up the money and started to play poker. This time it was Helen who spoiled it—she always knew when people were bluffing.

When they gave that up they started asking Uncle Grigorian questions. He wouldn't tell

them about the dispute in the Genic Sector because he was afraid he might make them biased. But he did tell them a bit about himself.

"Is Grigorian your real name?" Helen asked him.

"Yes. It sounds vaguely Eastern European, doesn't it?"

"What about your accent?"

"It's a Klipstian accent."

"Didn't it ever give you away, on Earth?"

"No. After all, if someone was really born in Poland, brought up in Germany, and living in Wales, who knows what sort of an accent he might have."

"How did you get your job?"

"Well, there are a lot of reasons. I'm a bit of a loner, for one thing. Klipst is a big planet with a small population, so we're not very gregarious creatures. But the main thing was that I'm so tall."

"Tall?" said Tubs. "You're almost a midget!"

"Tubs, you are rude!" said Helen.

"It's all right," Uncle Grigorian laughed. "That's something else I haven't told you about. Earth people are among the tallest people in the universe. Most humans are about five feet tall. I'm short by Earth standards, but tall by Galactic standards. Which means, incidentally, that you will be as tall as the average grown-up on Palassan."

They looked through the walls while they thought about that. Some of the staging posts they were passing through now were rooms on planets, rather than isolated points in space. They got occasional glimpses of weird creatures and strange cities, but the picture always faded before they could get a good look at it.

When, finally, the scene outside firmed up and stayed firm, they knew they were on Palassan.

Through the clear back wall of the office they saw a bearded man, a bit shorter than Helen and a bit taller than Fritz. He waited for a moment, then pushed at a section of the wall and stepped in.

Uncle Grigorian said, "This is Mr. Loman, Supervisor of Fringe Planets in the Galactic government. Mr. Loman, meet Helen, Fritz, and Tubs."

They all shook hands. Tubs said, "My name's Jonathan, by the way."

Helen could see that Mr. Loman's friendliness was only on the surface. Underneath, he was very wary of the children. He obviously knew they had Powers.

He rubbed his hands together and said, "We've got rooms all ready for you. Let's go, shall we?" He led them through the gap in the spaceship wall into a corridor, around a corner, and through a door.

They found themselves out in the open air. There was a clear sky and a small, hot sun. Fritz noticed a huge, pale moon near the horizon.

They were in some kind of park. Low, one-story buildings were dotted around the lawns, connected by narrow paths of pink gravel. It looked a bit like an RAF base Fritz had once visited.

Tubs said, "It doesn't look much like the capital of the galaxy."

"Is the whole planet like this?" Fritz asked.

"I like the smell of the grass," said Helen.

As they walked along one of the pink paths, Uncle Grigorian said, "Surely you didn't expect Palassan to look like London? Skyscrapers and traffic jams and crowded cities are a long way back in our past."

Mr. Loman added, "The government of the galaxy is just about the most important business there is. It has to be conducted in ideal surroundings. Peace and quiet, grass and trees—these things help administrators to think clearly.

"Of course, there are power stations and factories and so on here. However, we keep them underground, out of sight. And we don't need roads. People like Grigorian and myself—and you, now—go everywhere by Hypertrans. That's what we call the unit you got here in."

Fritz asked, "What about the people who work in the power stations and the factories?"

"Oh, there's a high-speed mechanical transport system underground," said Mr. Loman airily, as if to say that they need not worry their heads about that sort of thing. Fritz thought, but did not say, that it all sounded very well for the administrators but not so much fun for the public.

There were quite a lot of other people strolling around the paths and going in and out of the buildings. The ones who passed the children gave a nod and a pleasant smile.

Mr. Loman stopped at one of the low buildings. "We must take a photograph of you for the television newscast," he said. "Step inside for a moment."

They went into a wide hall lit by a forest of artificial lights. The brightness dazzled them for a moment.

When their eyes had adjusted, they made out a dozen or so of the short people. Most of them held pieces of equipment—cameras and things, Fritz guessed. Everything was much smaller than it would have been on Earth. There were no massive camera stands and floodlights, and none of the equipment had trailing cables.

One of the newspeople arranged the group of five in position, with Fritz shaking hands with Mr. Loman; and the cameras whirred for a few minutes. Then it was all over and they were outside again.

"We're celebrities," said Tubs. "Don't they want to interview me?"

Mr. Loman smiled. "I think we'll spare you all that," he said.

Helen began to wonder how anybody ever found their way around this place. All the buildings and the paths looked alike, and there were no signposts.

A girl stepped out of a doorway in front of them. She held a bunch of bright purple flowers in her arms. Helen thought they were lovely.

The girl must have seen Helen looking at them, for she picked one out and offered it. "The color suits you," she said with a bright smile. "Would you like one?"

Suddenly Tubs shot forward and knocked the flower out of the girl's hand.

"Tubs!" Helen protested.

The flower hit the ground with an unexpected tinkling sound, as if something had shattered.

"I'm so sorry," Helen said to the girl.

Mr. Loman grunted what sounded like a swearword.

Fritz picked up the flower and tore its petals off. Inside was some kind of electrical device.

The girl darted back into the doorway.

Uncle Grigorian brushed past Helen and opened the door the girl had gone through. There was no sign of her.

Mr. Loman had taken a leather case about the size of a match box out of his pocket and was speaking into it. "Young female, average height, pale blonde hair, Central Systems humanoid physical type, green tunic, carrying a bunch of Narchus flowers. Arrest and detain."

Helen asked, "What on earth is going on?"

Fritz showed her the shattered innards of the flower. "It looks like some kind of speaker for a radio," he said.

"A Whisperer," Uncle Grigorian said. "It repeats a message over and over, hypnotically. You can't hear it consciously, but it gets through to your subconscious. You end up believing it."

Fritz nodded. "Somebody wanted to hypnotize Helen—to get her to take their side in the dispute."

"But which side?"

Mr. Loman said, "We'll find out if we catch the girl."

They noticed that people were running across the lawns toward the spot where they stood. Most of them were men, dressed identically in dark red one-piece suits and matching skullcaps.

So they do have policemen on Palassan, Fritz thought.

Mr. Loman said, "The trouble is, she will certainly have changed her appearance. All she has to do is pull off that blonde wig and drop the flowers, and she's just like a thousand other young girls in the precinct."

"Come on," said Uncle Grigorian. "Let's leave this in the hands of the Redcaps. There's nothing we can do."

They reached the building where their quarters were to be. There were three bedrooms and a living room, all furnished in the plain, comfortable style of Uncle Grigorian's spaceship.

Mr. Loman pointed to a speaker on the wall by the door. "You can always speak to Grigorian or me just by pressing the button here," he said. "We'll leave you to unpack now."

"Well!" said Helen when they had gone. "It's just like a posh hotel."

Fritz pointed out through a window. Two of the Redcaps were standing outside. He went over and opened the door, and one of them walked toward him.

"Can I help you?" the Redcap said.

"No thanks," Fritz replied, and shut the door again. He turned to Helen. "Now what do you think it's like?"

"What on earth are you getting at?"

"To me it looks like a jail," said Fritz.

FIVE

· ·

THE WORM WAR

▼

*T*he next day they took the Hypertrans to another part of the planet. They had no way of telling how far they had gone, except that the sun was in roughly the same place when they arrived, so it could not have been very far. Uncle Grigorian went with them, and told them that the girl with the flowers had not been found. However, the Redcaps had found a bunch of flowers, a blonde wig, and a green tunic pushed into a corner.

While they waited for their course to be cleared by Hypertraffic Control, they watched themselves on a television newscast. The reporter said—

"Three primitives from a Fringe World in the Desic Sector arrived at Palassan yesterday in a last-ditch bid to solve the long-standing Worm War. Both sides have agreed in advance to accept the verdict of the alien adjudicators in a three-sided deal with the Galactic government. Hearings begin shortly under the supervision of government negotiator Swen Harliss, who is responsible for this unique attempt at an interplanetary reconciliation.

"The Vardic exploration mission: and a bulletin today says the team may have encountered—"

Uncle Grigorian switched the set off. "We're there," he said.

They stepped out of the Hypertrans into a wide, red-carpeted room with pictures on the walls. A slightly raised platform at one end bore three chairs and a low circular table. A white-bearded man in a black cloak was waiting.

"This is Swen Harliss," Uncle Grigorian said. Fritz wondered whether all the civil servants on Palassan wore beards, as a sort of badge of office.

There were two other people in the room. Harliss said, "Mr. Jaik and Mr. Karin represent the two sides in the dispute."

The two men nodded politely.

"What I plan to do is this," Harliss continued. "I will call up some expert witnesses to tell
you the background to the dispute; then our two
protagonists here can present their cases. Now,
if you will take your seats on the dais."

The twins and Tubs felt rather foolish as
they stepped onto the platform and sat down
around the low table. The room was much too
big for seven or eight people.

"The proceedings will be recorded on video-
tape, so that you will be able to play back any
part of the evidence later on," Harliss added.
"By the way, I thought you might like Grigorian
here to stay on, just so that you aren't entirely
among strangers."

"Yes, please," said Helen.

Uncle Grigorian took a seat beside the platform, and Harliss sat down in front of the children with Mr. Jaik and Mr. Karin on either side
of him. That left one empty chair: in between
the stage and the place where Harliss sat, at the
side of the room.

"I don't want to confuse you with a lot of
names," Harliss said. "The first expert is an astronomer."

The man who walked in was short even by
Palassan standards. His hair was white, but he
was clean-shaven. He wore the one-piece jump-
suit garment that most people on Palassan
seemed to have. He looked nervous.

He sat down in the empty chair and began to speak.

Four years ago the astronomer's research team at the University Planet had been studying star movements in the Genic Sector, at the far edge of the galaxy. The project had been a test of newly invented instruments for plotting the positions of planets. One set of observations had apparently been wrong: The orbits of all the planets around a very distant star had seemed to vary from the predicted path.

On checking, the team had found small variations in several other systems in the sector. At first, they had thought that a distant dark star, previously undiscovered, or an unknown planet in some of the systems must be responsible.

They had fed the figures into a computer and told it to describe the position of a star which would account for the variations—a large body which could be pulling the planets off course by means of gravity.

The computer had come up with a ridiculous result: a huge star in a place where everyone knew there was nothing but Deep Space.

One of the scientists had asked the computer another question: If a planet, rather than a star, was causing the freak orbits, where would its orbit lie?

The result had been just as ridiculous. The planet, the computer said, would be out in space, not attached to any of the stars.

Just to be thorough about the whole thing, the scientist had checked the position of the planet the computer had described.

It was there.

The discovery had caused quite a stir in astronomical circles. It was the first time anybody had found a wandering planet. Scientists had known that such things might exist, but there just didn't seem to be any.

Full details of the research work, and the calculations, were in the astronomer's paper to the Academy of Space Scientists, entitled "Some Anomalies in the Genic Sector."

When the astronomer stopped speaking, Harliss asked if there were any questions. Fritz said it was all perfectly clear. The astronomer left.

Harliss said, "The next witness is what we call a Rover. He's a kind of adventurer, traveling around unexplored sectors of space, partly for fun and partly for profit. There are thousands of them in the galaxy, roaming around in battered Hypertrans Units, hoping to make a quick fortune by discovering a solid gold meteorite or something. They earn their bread and butter by trading in a small way, and often smuggling.

"The Rovers are basically a nuisance. But they have their uses, as you'll see."

The Rover, when he came in, was a complete contrast to the astronomer. He wore thick, baggy trousers held up with a belt and a loose-fitting round-necked shirt. He walked awk-wardly, as if he was not used to gravity, and he seemed to resent having to tell his story to a bunch of civil servants and children.

"I was on a short skip from Geva to Tork," said the Rover, "loaded with molecular transistors. They turn 'em out in the billions on Geva, but they got no technology on Tork, so the Torkas pay fortunes for them. Anyhow, I was hyper-jumping blind, as usual. Out there, there's no preset routes where every landing point is safe— you just have to set the drive rough and hope there's nothing in the way when you arrive. That's what makes Rovin' dangerous, see.

" 'Course, I could have gone the preset route and played it safe. But it takes longer, and costs more. Then I would have had to charge the full price for the transistors on Tork, and bang goes my profit. That's what Rovin's all about, see. Every planet has a preset route to Palassan, so you can go anywhere if you go via Palassan. But if you go blind, you can save money and un-dercut the opposition.

"Anyhow, on the way to Tork I pick up this telecast on the hyperwaves. A stray planet no-body's ever heard of, out past the Genic Sector.

I look at the star map, such as it is, and I reckon I'm the nearest man in the galaxy to the stray planet.

"Well, what with a couple of bad jumps, it takes me a day or two. Then I find myself in orbit around this planet. Gave me a bit of a scare, I can tell you, to end up so close. Stars! A little bit farther and I would have landed smack in the middle of the thing, and whump! No more Rovin'.

"Still an' all, what with the planet having an atmosphere, and being so far from any star, I'm none the wiser 'cause I can't see nothin' but a gray blob. So down I goes, slowly, to the surface.

"I come up again pretty rapid, I can tell you. Them Worms could've ate me, unit and all, in one gulp. Lucky I could see 'em—there was some kind of light source under the clouds, and the surface was bright as day. All I see is loads of these Worms, one of 'em coming toward me, weaving this trail of stuff behind, and I'm gone.

"I should've gone straight on to Torka, I'll be frank. I never made nothin' out of the Worm World, 'cept a few guilders off the telecast people for the eyewitness story. No reward from the Galactic government for warning them. Huh. Anything else you want to know?"

There was nothing more the Rover could add,

and Harliss dismissed him with a look of relief.

The third witness was a Captain in the Space Fleet. Brown-skinned and clean-shaven, he wore a suit and skullcap just like the Redcap uniform, except that it was bright blue and had a white star on the breast. He had been in charge of the official expedition to the Worm World.

"The expeditionary force proceeded to the target planet in accordance with Imperial Order No. G65a/339, section—"

"Yes, yes, Captain, no need to go into that," said Harliss. "This isn't a formal hearing, you know. Just tell the story."

"Sir. The fleet halted within orbiting distance of said planet for preliminary observations. It was seen to be a Type Q body of unusually large mass. There was a small amount of atmospheric cloud, but apparently no large masses of water. There were no signs of intelligent life.

"On descending to the surface, the clouds were seen to be some kind of vegetable formation which emitted light. There was considerable animal life at zero altitude, consisting mainly of the caterpillarlike creatures which have become known popularly as, ahem, the Worms.

"They were approximately four meters in diameter, and their length varied from ten meters upward. They were seen to emit trails of a silklike substance as they moved about. Two important facts about these trails emerged. The first was that the trails followed some kind of geological subterranean pattern; the second, that the substance was in fact the complex plastic known as Unilon, which is manufactured on several worlds in the Central System.

"The Worms turned out to be nonaggressive and offered no resistance to capture. Several specimens of different sizes were dissected. Their brains were uniformly small, consisting mainly of a spinal cord.

"The planet's vegetation was simple and provided food for the Worms. However, a small proportion of the plant species were sensitive to stimuli of light and heat.

"More detailed investigation was outside the scope of the expeditionary force."

The Captain bowed stiffly and left. Harliss said, "That completes the background briefing. Is everything clear?"

Fritz leaned forward in his chair. "I think so," he said. "The Worm World is a stray planet, not attached to a sun of its own. It is populated by Worms, which feed on simple vegetation and spin Unilon. We still don't know what all the fuss is about."

"You will," said Harliss. "I'm now going to ask Mr. Jaik to speak."

Mr. Jaik had a thin face and a long nose. His green jacket bore a badge with the letters L.L. embroidered on it. He stood up.

"I am president of the League of Life," he said. "The League is supported by millions of humans throughout the galaxy. Quite simply, we are dedicated to the preservation of all forms of animal life throughout the universe.

"What you have not been told in your background briefing is what has happened to the Worm World since the Space Fleet came back with its report.

"You see, the substance the Worms spin—Unilon—is enormously valuable. Huge factories on several worlds produce the stuff at great cost. As soon as people discovered that there was a world of it, just waiting to be harvested, they descended on the Worm World in hordes.

"The first to arrive simply gathered up the Unilon in giant mechanical diggers and shipped it out. Later, more sophisticated methods were used. The Worms were forced to spin in straight lines to make the harvesting easier. In order to make them do this, an operation has to be done on their brains.

"Large areas of this world are now just Unilon factories, with slave Worms spinning up and down in straight lines all day and all night until they drop dead.

"The League of Life took over most of the Worm World in time to prevent the spread of this monstrous practice."

Harliss interrupted him. "I think you could stop for a moment, Mr. Jaik. I should now say that fighting broke out in several places along the borders of the League's property on the Worm World. The harvesters and the League's officers fought with handguns, and later with missiles. Each says the other side started it. The government stopped the fighting, and has been trying to arrange a truce ever since. That's why you're here. Now, perhaps Mr. Karin will tell you his side of the story."

Mr. Karin's face was rough and weather-beaten, a bit like the Rover's. He had a sheaf of papers under his arm, and Helen hoped he was not going to make a long speech.

He said, "I represent the Unilon Harvesters Association, which was formed by the workers of the Worm World to protect our rights.

"There are now a quarter of a million people, plus their wives and children, who depend upon the Worm World for their livelihood. The League of Lifers forget that when they talk about the poor caterpillars.

"It is just not true that the Worms suffer on our farms. They have all the food they want, and they are protected from disease and from predators.

"If the Worms are suffering, why don't they try to escape? The simple fact is, they are happy, in their little way. The League of Life is just a bunch of interfering busybodies with nothing better to do."

Harliss interrupted again. "Now, I will not let this hearing turn into a name-calling match." He looked up at the platform. "Have you any questions?"

"Just a minute," said Fritz. He turned to Helen and whispered, "I'm going to ask each of them a question. Watch them carefully." He turned back to the three men.

"Mr. Jaik, tell me, in one sentence, why you want to protect the Worms."

"I want to prevent cruelty and conserve the rich variety of animal life in the galaxy," replied Mr. Jaik.

"Mr. Karin, why are you against the League of Life?"

"It's my job to look after the jobs of two hundred fifty thousand workers," was the reply.

Fritz turned back to Helen. "Now," he whispered, "it's quite simple. Use your Power. Which of them is lying?"

"That's easy," said Helen. "They both are."

SIX

· ·

NIGHT FLIGHT

_____

▼

Helen was awakened by someone shaking her shoulder. She opened her eyes and saw Fritz.

"Get up," he said.

Helen looked at her watch. "It's the middle of the night!" she protested.

"Never mind. Get dressed. I'll wake Tubs."

Helen threw on her clothes. She could tell Fritz was not playing a joke. When she went into the living room of their little bungalow, Fritz was speaking on the intercom.

"What time is it in England?" he asked.

Uncle Grigorian's voice came through. "Just before midday."

"I think we should speak to Mum."

"Now?"

"Why not? We're all up."

"All right. I'll get a relay set up. It will take a couple of minutes."

Helen looked around the room. The table in the center was piled high with paperback books and videotapes. She asked Fritz, "Haven't you been to bed?"

"I've been doing a bit of research and found out some important things."

"Why do you want to speak to Mum?"

"We may not get another chance for a while."

Tubs came in with Glob on his shoulder. He never took the Petball off, these days. "What's going on?" he mumbled.

Through the intercom came the familiar sound of a telephone ringing. Uncle Grigorian's voice said, "You're through to Earth."

"Hello," said Mrs. Price.

"Hello, Mum," said Fritz.

"This is a nice surprise! Are you enjoying yourselves? Are you all right?"

"Fine," Fritz said. "Helen saw the lambs and Tubs and I drove the tractor. Uncle Grigorian thought we ought to call and tell you we're okay."

"That was thoughtful of him. Well, we mustn't run up a big bill. I've got to get on with the guests' lunches. Thank you for calling."

"Bye, Mum." Fritz turned away from the speaker.

"Now," he said to the others, "just leave all the talking to me." He went to the door and opened it. The Redcap on guard outside strolled over.

"I've left my games in Uncle Grigorian's Hypertrans," Fritz told him. "I'd like to go over and get them."

The Redcap frowned. "Can't it wait until morning?" he said. "You see, there's only one of us here at night. I'm supposed to guard you. If I stay here, you're all alone, and if I go with you, I have to leave the other two."

"That's no problem," said Fritz persuasively. "They can come, too. I'll need them to help carry some of the stuff, anyway."

"All right," said the Redcap. "Come on."

The lawns were lit by two moons, one big and silvery, the other small and yellow. The twins, Tubs, and the Redcap walked briskly along the gravel paths until they came to the place where they had arrived on Palassan.

The building was open, and they found their way to Uncle Grigorian's "office" without trouble. When they stepped inside Fritz pointed to the filing cabinet.

"The games are in there," he said.

"I don't know," the Redcap said with a grin. "You Earth people play games at funny hours."

Fritz opened the cabinet door and turned two switches.

"Hey!" shouted the Redcap.

The building outside the walls blurred and was gone.

"What have you done?" the Redcap said angrily.

"You can't operate a Hypertrans, can you?" Fritz said.

"No." The Redcap opened a pocket in his uniform and took out a small gun. "But you'd better take us back to Palassan quickly, or I'll blow your leg off."

Helen said, "Don't worry, Fritz. He's bluffing."

The Redcap looked frightened now. "Curse you," he muttered.

"Now, now. You can't make us go back to Palassan, so you'd better just settle down to the prospect of coming with us," Fritz said. "At least you can keep on protecting us this way. What's your name?"

"Arman."

"Fritz, will you tell us what you're up to?" Helen pleaded.

"Yes." Fritz made a couple of more adjustments to the dials. "These things are very easy to operate, once you've studied a star map," he said. "Now then. I've discovered quite a lot while you two have been snoring.

"First of all, I read up on the League of Life. Until three years ago, they were no more than a bunch of crackpots. Then, unexpectedly, they came into money and became a powerful body. This happened just after the Worm World was discovered.

"There's a law here that all charities have to declare where their money comes from. For the last three years, the League of Life has been getting big donations from something called the Gulben Trust. So I read up on the Gulben Trust. It gives money to all sorts of things—schools, research projects, famine relief, various charities."

"What's all this got to do with anything?" Tubs asked.

"Hang on a minute; I'm getting to the point. The Trust is run by a man called Jo Lee Olsom."

"Who's he?"

"Shut up, Tubs, and I'll tell you. He's retired now, but he used to be the boss of a company called Unilon Makers. Nowadays his sons run the business. And they've lost a lot of money since the cheap Unilon started coming out of the Worm World."

"I see!" said Helen. "In other words, the League of Life is paid by Unilon Makers to make trouble for the Worm World."

"Exactly," said Fritz. "But that's not all. I've also been looking up the Unilon Harvesters Association, and they're just as bad. They don't represent the workers of the Worm World, at all. It's not like a trade union, with elected officials and so on. It's a publicity body, owned by the three men who run all the Worm farms."

Tubs said, "So far as I can see, nobody's being honest with us."

"In a nutshell, yes," Fritz replied. "So we've got to start from scratch."

"So where are we going?" Helen asked.

"To the Worm World," said Fritz, and turned back to his dials.

They landed on the wild side of the world which had been taken over by the League in order to keep the Farmers away from it. Fritz used a preset route right up until the last hop, which he did blind, like the Rovers.

They arrived smack in the middle of a herd of Worms.

The creatures were enormous—much bigger than whales. They looked more like caterpillars than worms, for they had tiny legs at the base of each segment. They had black, multifaceted eyes at the front. As they crawled about, a thick rope of Unilon emerged from underneath them.

The four people in the Hypertrans looked through the transparent walls with horrified fascination.

Helen said: "Every so often, they change direction abruptly. It's as if . . . as if they were following a trail."

Arman spoke. He had been silent for most of the journey, sitting down with a sulky look on his face. But the Worm World made him forget he was supposed to be in a bad mood. "Maybe they're looking for food," he suggested.

"It's not that kind of movement," Helen said.

"The Captain said it had something to do with rocks and stuff underground," Tubs remembered.

Fritz looked below. "They lay a kind of network of Unilon," he said. "It looks complex enough to be *for* something—to have a purpose—but . . ." He trailed off.

"I'm going outside," Tubs said.

"Oh, no you don't." Arman had remembered his job again.

"Let him," Fritz said. "The Worms are harmless—we know that."

Tubs opened the section of wall which served as a door. His face looked rather white, but he put on a show of boldness. "Here goes!" he said, and stepped out.

He sniffed the air, turned around, and gave an exaggerated shrug for the benefit of the twins. He took a few paces forward, and bent down to touch a length of Unilon.

"Ouch!" he said, and pulled his hand back quickly.

"What happened?" Helen called out anxiously.

"It tingles," Tubs said.

Fritz was excited. "Like an electric shock?"

"Yes." Tubs came back into the Unit. "What do you think that means?"

"I don't know," said Fritz, "but it means something." He opened the filing cabinet.

"Shall we move on?" Helen suggested. "I'd like to look at the stuff the Worms feed on."

"Great minds think alike," Fritz replied. "Here we go."

He moved the Hypertrans across the surface of the planet in small hops until they came across a vast flat prairie of dark green plants. They had big saucer-shaped leaves which pointed to the sky like radar receivers.

"Now," said Fritz. "The Captain said this vegetation was sensitive to light and heat. I wonder just what he meant."

"I suppose, if you shine a flashlight on them, they turn toward it," said Helen. "Let's try that."

"Who's got a flashlight?" Fritz asked. "Arman?"

"Yes." Arman had gotten interested in the planet now. He unzipped a pocket and brought out a tiny pencil flashlight.

Fritz opened the door and shined the flashlight into the center of one of the saucer-shaped

leaves. Gradually, he moved the beam across to the rim of the leaf. It did not move.

"Bang goes that theory."

"Hmm. Not necessarily, Helen. Let me try something else." He took out his penknife and sawed through the stalk of the plant. When it came free, he looked at the cut stem and prodded it with his finger.

"So far, so good," he said. "See?" He showed it to the others. "There's a core of some hard stuff running through the plant. Now."

Fritz unscrewed the cap of the flashlight and took out the bulb. "Got a cigarette lighter, Arman?"

Arman unzipped another pocket and passed Fritz his lighter.

"Right," said Fritz. "The lighter will provide both heat and light." He flicked on the flame and held it close to the surface of the leaf. Then he took the flashlight bulb and touched its base to the hard core in the stem of the plant.

The bulb flickered on.

"That's it!" Fritz shouted. "Heat and light on the surface of the leaf generate electricity in the plant."

"Good," said Arman. "Can I have my lighter and my flashlight, please?"

Fritz handed them over. "It's a system, don't you see?" he said. "The plants generate electricity—the Unilon is electrified. The Worms feed on the plants and make the Unilon. It all fits together—but what's it for?"

"I'm hungry," said Tubs.

"Me, too," said Helen. "And poor Arman looks very uneasy. Why don't we go across to the Farmers' side of the planet?"

"Fine," said Fritz. "We may get some answers there."

SEVEN

· ·

THE EARTHQUAKE CLUE

_____

▼

They stopped at the edge of a small town. The cloud above was feeble and gave very little light. It was cold.

The place reminded Tubs of a film he had seen about gold-mining towns in Alaska. There were rickety prefabricated houses, unpaved roads, and scruffy shops.

Hurrying to keep warm, they made their way toward the town center and looked for a cafe.

It seemed there was no Hypertrans or underground railway here. Electric cars, like high-speed golf carts, tore around the streets. Many of the people wore fur hats.

Fritz had a thought. "Have you got any money?" he asked Arman.

"Yes. Not much, but enough for a meal."

"What about the currency—will it be different?"

"No. This is a brand new world—no time for them to develop their own money. They'll speak Galingua like us, too."

Several people stared unpleasantly at Arman. Eventually he said, "I don't think Redcaps are very popular here."

"You'd better disguise yourself," Helen suggested. "Fritz, give him your jacket."

"I'll freeze!"

"It's not for long. There. Now, Arman, take off your cap." She looked at the result. "Now you're just a man in red trousers."

Soon they saw a brightly lit window. Through it they could see tables and chairs and a few people eating. They went in and sat down.

The man behind the counter called out, "You want a meal, or just coffee?"

"A meal," Arman said, speaking for all of them. "What've you got?"

"Stew, stew, or stew," said the man.

"I guess we'll take the stew. Four times."

The man brought four big bowls and four spoons. "Ten credits," he said as he plunked the food on the table.

"What!" said Arman incredulously. "That ought to buy four thick steaks."

"This is the Worm World, brother. Ten credits."

Arman paid up reluctantly, and they started to eat.

"I wonder what's in it," said Tubs.

"Well, the green bits are presumably the vegetable stuff," Fritz guessed.

"So what's the meat? It tastes good."

"I'll give you three guesses," said Fritz. "I mean, what else is there on this planet except vegetation?"

"Worms," said Tubs.

"There's your answer."

"Ugh." Helen pushed her plate away.

The man at the next table leaned over toward them. "You're new here," he said.

Helen looked at him. She could not be sure whether he was growing a beard or had just stopped shaving for a few days. He wore a battered hat and there was a tooth missing in the front.

"Yes, we're new," Helen said.

"They didn't tell you about the food, eh?" The man laughed mockingly. "They never do."

"You're an old-timer, are you?" she asked.

"Yep. Been here three years. I was with the first shipload of dupes."

Fritz put in, "Anything else they forgot to mention, old-timer?"

He chortled again. "Just about everything. The earthquakes, for beginners. Then there's the cost of everything, especially your passage back home. Oh, they tell you about the wages all right. A hundred credits a week, plus bonus! Then you find out a bowl of Worm stew costs two-fifty, and—"

"What's this about earthquakes?" Fritz interrupted. He had stopped eating, and he gazed intently at the man.

"Oh, they come along every few months, knock all the houses down, maybe kill a few people. Sometimes they're big, sometimes not so. The only way to be safe 'n sure is to live in a Hypertrans—don't nothing move them. That's where all the foremen live. Yes, sir!"

"Do they know what causes the earthquakes?"

"Folks say it's electrical, but nobody really knows. Everything falls down, so we build it up again—"

Fritz was not listening anymore. He was slapping his knee with delight and whispering, "That's it! That's it!" Arman was looking at him intently.

"Out with it then," Helen prompted him.

"That's what the electricity's for. Isn't it obvious? The electricity from the plants goes through the Unilon and down into the core of the planet. The electricity shifts the rock about and causes the earthquakes. That's how the planet moves."

"I don't understand that," said Helen.

"Me neither," said Tubs.

Fritz thought for a minute. "Have you ever seen the old men playing lawn bowling on the green in the park at home? Well, the balls they roll are biased—they're heavier on one side than the other. That causes them to roll in a curve instead of a straight line.

"Now, if the heavy matter in the center of a planet were to shift about, it would make the planet curve—right? So the earthquakes would direct the motion of the Worm World."

Helen said, "I follow all that, but I don't see why it's such a great discovery."

Arman said, "I'm afraid I do." His voice had changed, and Helen looked at him, surprised. Then she saw that his little gun was in his hand.

"Get up and leave here quietly," he said. "I mean business this time."

Fritz looked at Helen. She said, "He's not bluffing now."

Baffled, the three children stood up and walked out, with Arman behind them. The old-timer gave them a puzzled look and returned to his meal.

Arman marched them down the road to a

big stone building. Inside, he showed a glowing square like a badge or an identity card to an official behind a desk.

"I want to put these three in a cell," he said.

The official seemed scared by the sight of the card. "Yes, sir!" he said. "This way, sir."

They were put into a tiny room with a barred window and a spy hole in the door. Arman stood in the doorway, his gun still on them.

"I can't help admiring you," he said in his new, confident voice. "You figured it all out in an incredibly short time. But we can't have the rest of the galaxy finding out, can we?"

"No, you can't," Fritz said dully.

"You've even worked out that I'm a secret agent for the farm owners, haven't you?"

Fritz nodded.

Helen gasped. "Why didn't I suspect you? My Power should have—"

Arman smiled. "You knew I was uneasy, didn't you?"

"Yes, but I thought you were frightened of the Worm World—oh, I've been so stupid!" She banged her fist against her forehead in exasperation.

"Settle down and practice being good losers," said Arman, and shut the cell door.

Helen looked at Fritz. "What is it that you and Arman understand, and Tubs and I don't?"

"I'll go through it again," said Fritz. "The

planet draws energy from the stars—or the sun, when it's near one—through the plants. They turn sunlight into electricity. The electricity passes through the Unilon into the center of the planet, where it causes enormous shifts of weight which move the planet. I knew there was something about the network of Unilon. But now I see. The Unilon is a brain. The Worm World is alive. The whole planet is one big animal!"

Understanding dawned on Helen's face. "Why not? It can think, it can move itself, it feeds on sunlight, it can heal if it's damaged: I take it that's what the Worms do, heal damaged brain sections?"

"Yes, that fits, too. The caterpillars are controlled by small movements of earth just below the surface. Yes."

Tubs butted in. "Look, this is all very well, but—" He stroked Glob, as if seeking comfort. "But how does Arman fit in?"

"I'm sure the Farmers have already discovered the truth about the Worm World. Now, think a bit. The planet could not possibly get enough energy from starlight to move these great masses of rock. It needs a sun close by. Presumably, it's looking for one right now. I suppose it will home in on the nearest. It will throw all the other planets in the system off course—and if a planet goes out of orbit, human life there is almost certain to be destroyed. You know, ice caps melt and flood everything, crops burn up, and so on.

"As soon as the government finds out about the Worm World, it will want to blow it up. After all, they have to put human life first. So the Farmers are trying to keep it a secret, so that they can get as much Unilon as possible out of the place before the truth gets out. Arman was a spy, planted on us by the Farmers, to get us out of the way if we found out." He added bitterly, "We played right into his hands."

In a quiet voice Tubs asked, "Is there anything we can do now?"

"First we've got to get out of here."

"Then?"

"Then we've got to talk to the planet."

EIGHT

· ·

ALL FALL DOWN

▼

*T*here was a distant rumbling noise, like thunder, or trucks on a superhighway. Fritz looked up, and the others followed his gaze. The light bulb which hung by a cord from the ceiling was swaying to and fro. As they looked, a long crack appeared in the plaster.

"Under the bed!" Fritz yelled.

The three of them dived underneath the iron-framed single bed which stood against one wall of the cell. The rumbling seemed to get nearer.

"It's an earthquake!" Tubs gasped. He stroked Glob.

The floor seemed to lift and sway. Lumps of plaster and fragments of stone fell on the bed

and the floor around it. The noise became deaf-
ening. There were screams from somewhere else
in the building, and the sound of a man shouting.
Helen covered her ears with her hands and
closed her eyes tightly in terror.

It seemed to go on for ages. Then, suddenly,
everything was quiet. Helen opened her eyes.

"Are you all right?" she whispered.

"Just about," said Tubs.

"Yes," said Fritz. "Look!" He pointed.

Helen followed the direction of his finger—
and saw the street outside. The wall of their cell
had a huge hole in it.

They scrambled out from under the bed,
picked their way across the rubble in the cell,
and crawled out through the hole. They looked
around for a moment to get their bearings; then,
without speaking, they all began to run along
the road out of the town.

It could not have been a very bad earthquake,
they could tell. Some of the wooden buildings
had collapsed, but the brick and stone structures
were still standing, although damaged. Every
window was broken, including the big one at
the cafe where they had eaten Worm stew.

Nobody bothered with them in the confusion. People were helping the injured, inspecting
the damage, and looking through the wreckage
for bodies. However, Arman's first thought

would probably be to check on his prisoners, so they had no time to spare.

They came upon the Hypertrans, on a patch of waste ground past the last building of the town, and dived in. Fritz went straight to the controls. The world outside faded, and they were on the move.

Fritz drove in short hops again. "I'm looking for a nice patch of light-sensitive vegetation," he muttered.

Helen asked, "Did you mean that, about talking to the planet?"

"Yes," he said curtly. He was concentrating on the dials.

"But what language will you use?"

"Morse code," he said. "Ah. This will do."

He stopped the Hypertrans and looked around. They were in a field of vegetation. A herd of Worms munched contentedly over a mile away. Up above, the cloud gave a steady, dim light.

"Help me roll up the carpet," said Fritz.

Mystified, the others got down on the floor and lifted the edges of the gray carpet. As they rolled, they moved the furniture off the carpet and onto the bare, transparent floor.

Fritz stood by the light switch. "Here goes," he said. He switched the light off for a moment; then flashed it on, three times.

Nothing happened.

He did it again.

Still nothing.

He said, "If the planet really has a brain, I was hoping it would recognize a regular pattern. The lights in here are quite powerful—but perhaps too dim for such a big brain to notice." He looked disappointed.

"How will you know if it does recognize the signal?" Helen asked.

"Look!" said Fritz by way of reply. They all looked up at the sky.

The light-cloud above brightened, then dimmed, three times.

"See? We can talk to it." Fritz flashed the Hypertrans lights four times, and the cloud flashed four times in response.

"Now," said Fritz, "we have to work out a common language."

Helen said, "I'll leave you to it. I'm dead beat." She settled into a chair, closed her eyes, and went to sleep.

The clack-clack of the typewriter on Uncle Grigorian's desk woke her. She glanced at her watch and saw that she had been asleep for five hours. Tubs snored quietly in the chair beside her.

Fritz was sitting at the desk, banging at the

typewriter with two fingers. The Hypertrans lights flashed on and off continuously. The typewriter was connected by a tangle of wires to the filing cabinet, the light switch, and one of the saucer-shaped leaves out in the field.

"What on earth are you doing?" Helen mumbled sleepily.

Fritz looked very tired, but exhilarated. His face was pale and drawn, but his eyes flashed with enthusiasm. "I've programmed the computer in there," he said, pointing at the filing cabinet, "to translate what I type into flashes.

"When the planet wants to talk back to me, it makes the cloud flash. The leaf out there picks up the flashes from the cloud, feeds them into the computer, and the computer types out the words on here."

"What have you found out?"

"The planet is dying—we've got to save it."

Tubs woke up.

"Listen, both of you," said Fritz. "I was right about the planet looking for a sun. It's starving—its reserves of power are running out. But when the Farmers came, and made the Worms spin straight lines, it was like a drug to the planet. Its brain went to sleep. When I flashed the lights at it, it had the same effect as an alarm clock. I woke the planet up. We've got to let the government know."

"But I thought you said the government will blow the planet up," Tubs said.

"I've made a deal with the planet," said Fritz. "It will allow the Farmers to work certain parts of its surface, and produce a limited amount of Unilon. In return, I've promised that the Galactic government will find it a sun—one which hasn't got any inhabited planets in its system.

"That way the farmers are happy and the planet is happy. Even the Unilon manufacturers on the other worlds will be all right, because there won't be enough Unilon made on the Worm World. Unilon is used in loads of things—clothes, machines, and so on. They'll still make a profit."

"That's tremendous," said Helen.

"But I think it's too late," said Tubs. "Look out there."

Across the field, two or three miles away, a line of electric cars was advancing. As they watched, a bright flash came from one of the cars, and the vegetation between the cars and the Hypertrans was scorched.

"The Farmers, they're attacking us!" said Fritz.

"Let's Hyperjump—quick!" Tubs shouted.

"Can't. I've reprogrammed the computer. It would take ages to put it together again."

The typewriter began to clack. The children

rushed over to see what it said. They read:

WHAT WAS THAT

Fritz thought for a minute, then typed:

i am being attacked

"We haven't got around to punctuation yet," he explained. The typewriter clacked on.

WHO ATTACKS

unilon farmers

CAN YOU FIGHT UNILON FARMERS

no

The typewriter went silent. There were more shots from the electric cars, and the scorched vegetation was nearer this time.

"What are the Worms doing?" said Tubs.

They all looked. The herd of Worms, which had been peacefully grazing a moment before, was now on the move. The great beasts lumbered about in apparent confusion for a few minutes. Then the children saw that they were forming a line.

The monsters lumbered slowly toward the Farmers.

The shots were aimed at the Worms now, but although some of them landed, the Worms ignored them.

Some of the electric cars stopped; then, one by one, they all did.

The leading Worm reached a car. In the distance, the children saw its great mouth open wide. The mouth swallowed the car, and the Worm lumbered on.

The rest of the cars turned around and fled.

"Blimey!" said Fritz.

Suddenly there was another Hypertrans beside theirs. Uncle Grigorian stepped out of it. Helen ran to him and flung her arms around his neck.

"Thank goodness you're here," she said. She began to cry.

"There, there," said Uncle Grigorian. "My word, it took a long time to find you three. What in the galaxy have you been up to?"

They were back in the red-carpeted room with pictures on the walls. After a meal, a bath, a night's sleep, and another meal, they all felt as good as new. Helen had forgotten all about Worm stew.

Swen Harliss was saying, "The Farmers and the Unilon Makers have accepted the compromise negotiated by Fritz, I'm happy to say. A team of scientists has taken over the rather splen-

did communication link set up in the Hyper-trans, and they are at present talking to the planet. They hope to learn a lot from it.

"Meanwhile, our astronomers have found a suitable sun for the Worm World to orbit around." He pointed to a star map on a table. "It's here, in the Parmic Sector. It can be reached without the Worm World going dangerously close to any other solar systems. It already has two planets, but neither has an atmosphere, let alone any life on it. Your job is done, and very well, too. Now, what would you like to do?"

They looked at each other, and then at Uncle Grigorian. Tubs spoke for all of them.

"Can we go home?" he asked.

It was early morning when they got back to the farmhouse, and Mrs. Rhys prepared the usual huge breakfast.

As they sat in the familiar surroundings of the kitchen, the events of the last few days began to seem like a dream. Every so often Tubs would stroke Glob, as if to reassure himself that it had all really happened.

"Of course, you will always have your Powers," said Uncle Grigorian as he lit his pipe. "You're all going to have to be very grown-up about using them." He paused, and puffed away for a minute. "Still, I think you have grown up a lot in the last week.

"Fritz—you must be very clever about things like games. If you beat everybody hands down at everything, it will go to your head. And nobody likes a bighead. So lose at chess from time to time, just to prevent people from becoming suspicious.

"Helen—you've learned how to tell what's going on in people's minds. It's not always pleasant to know that sort of thing. You're going to find out how nasty people can be. You must practice being sympathetic.

"Tubs—I don't know what you're going to do with Glob. I don't suppose they'll let you take him to school. Still, he'll be happy enough without you all day if he sees you every evening. Put him on a shelf in your bedroom and tell people he's an ornament."

They all nodded seriously. It was rather a long speech for Uncle Grigorian to make.

"Well!" he said, and his solemn look was replaced with his usual mischievous grin. "What would you like to do today?"

"How about another driving lesson?" said Fritz.

For some reason, Uncle Grigorian found that funny. He laughed and laughed until his pipe went out.